NEXT STOP ETERNITY

poems by

Susan Glyn

Published by Feather Books
Fair View, Old Coppice, Lyth Bank,
Shrewsbury SY3 OBW, U.K.
Tele/fax; 01743 872177

Website URL: http://www.waddysweb.com
e-mail: john@waddysweb.freeuk.com

1999

1st Edition July 1999
2nd Edition September 1999

ISBN 0 947718 94 X

No. 69 in the Feather Books Poetry Series

CONTENTS

page

INTRODUCTION

SUSAN GLYN belongs to a family of writers. She is descended from Alaw Goch, Welsh bard and poet; married the author Anthony Glyn and was the mother of novelist and poet Caroline Glyn. She never went to school, but wrote poetry from childhood. She has also been an anti-aircraft gunner, philosophy student, barrister and sculptor.

Her poems have been published in many periodicals and anthologies. Her first collection was published by "Outposts" poetry quarterly.

Susan Glyn's themes are derived from her Christian faith and in this sequence she reflects on the great adventure of moving from this world to the next.

WHEN TIME HAS LOST ITS ARROW
Events and noises round us seem unreal,
(and our near future best forgotten).
All beyond that is over our horizon.
So Time has lost its arrow.

The past is now the present; all its scenes
more vividly experienced than a mere yesterday.
Each memory is NOW.
And there's no sequence;
they're shuffled like a pack
dealt us in any order.
Involuntary in recall.

All the surprise of life's still there.
What next? We still don't know
what times, the glad or sad, we must relive.
The question's still unanswered:
which is the stronger, joy or suffering?
Like T.V. Channels fighting for our minds.
We try to total them, and then decide
"Was our life good?" - But there's no summing up.

Meanwhile, the scenes detach and reassemble.
Each fragment independent, moving
into one time, a single fabric
of many elements. A great mosaic.
Taking on shape itself, revealing
our roots and branches to us;
its structure that we never saw before;
its balance; all the beauty, of this still-growing tree,
our personal, once-and-future Tree of Life.

THE TURNING-POINT

You go up and up, with a fierce joy that's new.
Excitement growing as you tread and tread.
A path so steep it seems to scrape your face.
The whole great mountain seeming part of you,
holding you with its strength, forcing the pace,
until you struggle up and reach the crown,
and find there's only sky over your head.

No wonder you lie there and clutch the summit.
You know it's always harder coming down,
to keep your footing as you slide and plummet.
There's no more hand-hold; you can't see your heel.
You toil on when you're tired, and luck's run out.
It's fear now, not adventure that you feel.
You wonder why you climbed; - *what life's about.*
It's only then that you can see the view.

THREE ETERNITIES (In the Alpes Maritimes)
Turn left for Eternity.
That little gate leads down towards the sea.
The land-horizon ranges high above;
the mountain path turns right,
out of the other door, towards the hills.

I'm circled by the edges of our world.
Cradled, perhaps, because I'll sleep on through,
beyond all these horizons, in the end.
And, until then,I can enjoy this dream;
a moment held in time. My first eternity.

CITY FOG

There is nothing there.
This is the empty air,
whose clearness streamed unsensed
through my whole being;
only the ear aware
of its sound-laden causeway
linking the nearness
of the breathing city.

Now there is silence.
Air grown dense,
its unseen content charged
at some unheeded flashpoint
sandpapers every sense,
and I'm alone,
choking and blinded, cold,
the city gone.

Within this air, entwined
closer through heart and mind
than all the web of air-red arteries,
tangible, suddenly I find
another atmosphere opaque to me,
pressing on will, emotion, destiny,
as tides of a weighted sea,

Currents of every age
from time's revolving stage;.
growing and sinking rhythms of race
and place, outlasting time;
eddying fashion's rage.
And every thought that is, or was
conceived; all that has type or name;
layer on layer, soup-thick to the stars.

Awareness is too sudden.
Skies overladen
crush down life and will;
the fugue, too loud,
joins my heart's beat, its burden
intolerably thudding
in thought and blood,
the self invading.

Beyond earth's atmosphere
the vanished stars, frost-clear,
disallow my appeal
from the drowning air -
only in death swing near.
Afraid, I grope once more
down the fog-filled street
to my own door.

As I go in
I can breathe again.
And all the world's shut out.
And the desired, quiet star,
shielded within,
inviolate,
I find, where the air is clear,
the candle lit.

THE REMISSION

It's no use being "half-in-love
with easeful death"; - that door has slammed.
Perhaps for several years, they say.
Where am I now? With life to start again
and all the old paths barred behind me.

"Just don't overdo things." - Meaningless advice.
Overdo what? Can "Nothing" be overdone?
Multiply three hundred and sixty five by nought
and you're still at zero... zero... a nought... an egg?
Eggs hatch. But then what birds, what years, what flights
are in me still? Days void, long nightmare nights,
are all I find. But, wait...Someone's been here before.
Someone came back and faced it all again.

Oh, Jesus, give me grace to follow You.
Then I shall know what *You* want me to do.

IF THE WORLD'S YOUR ORANGE
don't get earthbound. Keep the surface out of it!
That clutter of things all round.
Don't break your teeth on indigestible stuff;
matter doesn't matter a bit,
enough's enough.

Why chew the rind,
when all the fruit's within?
Juice in the mind.

("The Kingdom of God is within you.")

SHARING THE CROSS

Only one man helped Jesus when He needed it most.
The stranger, Simon, picked on in the street
to share in carrying the cross.
Long afterwards he must have understood
the privilege he'd had.
But not just then.

As we grow old, our cross is built inside us;
made of our crumbling bones.
And we don't choose it either.
We carry it the whole Way-of-the-Cross
but in slow motion.
And no one sees or knows the pain it costs.
Can we suppose that if we bear it well
we're carrying just some splinter of the cross -
sharing with Jesus?

POETRY

The humblest Muse of all,
like lichen in a wall,
lives in interstices of life.
But there its rhythm grows
levering blocks apart
till chinks of light come through.
Stronger than stone
as cities turn to lace.

And we are weightless
if our memories hold
the verses from our life,
transforming still,
when we are very old.

Companions of the grave,
even inscribed in darkness;
there catacombs are honeycombs
filled and distilled with gold.

THE MIGHT-HAVE-BEENS.

I'm thinking backwards down my stream of life.
Meeting at each cross-roads that Might-have-been,
that other me, who took the other path;
taking away, each time, a part of me.
How strange to meet again and find them friends;
at the end, too, like me, of all their roads,
and coming back, one by one, to join me.
I know them all, - the soldier, artist, lawyer,
                              even philosopher,
who once were part of me, each my potential;
each one discarded at some different parting,
to leave myself as poet; so unlike the rest.

Were they existing, too, in all this time?
Living their life in some alternative world?
Or was I, all along, playing "Sardines"
With all my hidden selves, the might-have-beens?
I feel a strange fulfilment, a new wholeness,
now that we've joined again,
like facets of a diamond. Which is true?
Only the whole is real, when we are born anew.

THE HOLLOW

In the palm of a hand,
hollowed between the curves
of the sea's dark horizon and the hills,
I am at rest, in a great stillness,
sheltered from storms of this tempestuous earth.

Learning what quiet is.
          Play no music!
I want to hear the quiet.
          Make no movement!
I want to feel the hills.
And listen, until I know Whose hand
contains me. And Whose stillness
is at the centre of the world.
In which I am helpless now,
but need no help but His.

Who will come in His own time
to deliver me. Our time has vanished here
and has no meaning. I must wait on His.

He will come, I think, when I have learnt His peace.

THE SUM OF THE PARTS

I've sent myself forward, luggage in advance,
one package at a time,
to an unknown station.

First it was my legs,
and then my strength.
But I was still here then,
still being Me.

Then there was more to send:
my sight, my memory, my taste.
And almost all my breath.
Still I was Me.

At last it was my mind. I felt it go.
It all meets up, I know,
parts reassembled, living.
But now I don't ask *where*
but *Who* I'm going to find.

BIRTH AND REBIRTH

How long a baby spends, waiting for birth.
Kicking about, just growing, and maybe thinking;
dreaming his life on earth.
And how long, as life ends, we wait for death.
Shuffling about, just knowing; while life is shrinking.
Feeling our failing breath.
Knowing so many things. Yet unaware
what privilege to find in this repose,
unharnessed from the world and all its care.
What essence to distil from many griefs?
      And no-one knows
how to re-weave the shreds of our beliefs.
But griefs will be transmuted in clairvoyance.
To see, we need the eyes of our Redeemer.
What seeds may germinate then, from our experience,
which He will bring to life, in our next Spring?
Now we can change from sufferer to dreamer,
and lean on Him, in this as everything.

JUMPING OFF THE WORLD

Over the horizon; (feet first for a long jump).
Like Cortez, looking with "a wild surmise".
Or else, despairing, filled with learned lies.
Or just prepared to see with our own eyes.
Ready for a bump.

Ships never got there;
just went round and round. Earthbound.
The sea's unchanging change, and no escape,
till some far-off landscape
with quite familiar shape.
A New World all too like the old.

We need our wings to fly
into the vivid sky.
Astronauts try; -
living in slum-motels, they can't say why.
Coming back tired and older, with a sigh.

But wings!- We had them once.
In dreams we all remember. We could glide,
feet never on the ground: the world so wide
there wasn't a horizon.
That can't have been illusion.
When life runs out, we'll have to trust the angels
to lend their wings, until we find our own,
and fly into the deep of the Unknown.

ROSES

So many memories mingled, in a bowl of roses.
As I lean over, drinking in their scent,
they fill my mind with scenes of long ago.
The pink bud, for my father's buttonhole,
when I was eight years old; the verse I wrote him: -
    "A single rose can give us boundless pleasure,
    For rose means love, and love no man can measure."
He wiped his glasses. Kept my verse for ever.

Red; a huge bowl of them, in the "Bec Rouge"
In Monte Carlo. Their headwaiter thrust
the lot into my arms, as we went out.
Romantically we strewed them in our bed.
(Don't try it, they have thorns).

White roses for the bride. White roses on her grave.
She went so young to God, taking Him all her freshness.
Herself a rose.

Yellow, in massive bunches, for our Golden Wedding.
So soon before our parting.

And now, beside my bed, the blue dusk fills them.
Petals curl over shadow, and their shapes
are lost in a new music, like our own.
Still beautiful, but now ethereal,
weaving old memories into radiant vision.
In death's embrace we find the Mystic Rose.

THE LAST FAREWELL

After your car, your daughter and your wife,
(whichever order you may put them in),
there's still the parting with your life,
your body, which has been your friend.
Adding a lot to pleasures; sharing knocks;
and seeming to deserve a better end
than sending for scrap, in such an ugly box.

After a lifetime, no handshake, no pension.
Just to be left, fighting in bitter tension
against dismissal. What a breach of trust!
Peace only heals you when you come to terms:-
promise the immortality of dust,
the other ticket to life, beyond the worms,
but not on the same train. It's still goodbye.

THE LONG HOME

Somewhere to lay his head,
in the soft new-turned ground.
The companionship of the earth,
with mingled future and past.
Woven and interwoven
in the roots of the grass above
whose seeds will visit the sun
and return, new but unchanged,
to a quiet, where the only music
is the pulse of the world.
Where the stranger and wanderer, at last,
takes seisin of his land.

TO A SCIENCE LECTURER

"Heat lost," you say, "is equal to heat gained."
"Through changing forms all
energy's retained."
You prove no grain of dust can
cease to be.
Why grant no immortality to me?

To my Gunnery Instructor, who said: -

"THE TRAJECTORY OF A PROJECTILE IS INVARIABLY A PARABOLA"

As straight as an arrow!
Its flight curves in fall.

We may reach for the skies
but Earth-mother will call.

"Stand up straight!" - spines are curved;
we bow out, after all.

Yet some spark will shoot upward,
released from THE FALL.

JUDGEMENT

Repent? Of course I don't!
Because I don't know, yet, why I'm accused.
It's a blank form to fill up for myself.

That's unfair! "Sins I know not of "?
and "Things I left undone"?
Black marks against me that I never knew

when I was doing fine. Or so I thought.
Or did I? Have I ever thought?
      Or even thought I *ought*?

      I'll score myself a nought.

HELL

He didn't have time to change.
Just came in as one of the rest.
He'd been cold in his mother's arms,
but not this ultimate cold
and positive, utter dark.
Only faces with corpse-like glimmer
and eyes seeing only Death.

Some of them knew him and laughed.
"So you've decided to join us?"
"Bit of a come-down for you?"
"No surprise! I saw through you all along."
But a woman touched him. "You're new.
You've got earth-light on you still.
I came in without a rag on me, too.
You'll get used to it being bad."

"For your mercy, you shall be saved."

"There isn't a way out of here."

"I am the Way. Look into my eyes."

Then everything changed.

MOUNTAIN AFTER-GLOW

Even more magical than dawn.
in the high mountains, is the after-glow.
When the sun sets behind the heights
and then the day's reborn.
There's a blue darkness, then the scene relights.
Fingers of lilac shadow curve on snow,
but peaks rise up in flame
and every ridge and shoulder catches fire.
A light to blind us,
in frosty cold, yet burning all the same,
engulfing us, like Pompeii, with its flow.

When it's our time to know
that our encounter's past with Ice-Man Death;
our sun was lost; he slowly froze our breath;
and all the valley's dark; it's night behind us.
That mountain scene remains the true reality.
We can await in faith the after-glow.
Then ogres Night, Cold, Death lose their finality.

VISION

When the whole world becomes transparent,
lit from within,
we know we're free;
seeing as angels see,
distilled from sin.
The beauty of the earth is now transcendent,
our sight is clear
again, and all our mind.
How strange to find
that we can hear,
and all our strife's forever left behind.

(A personal vision during a Christmas-Eve service)

THE FIRST SUPPER

I looked up, and my sight went through the roof,
beyond the Cross and beams, into the night -
then through the night as well.
For there "shall be no night".

A group of men, with eager, smiling eyes,
and a deep joy, were pressing forward;
behind them, a great crowd, to greet their guest.
I recognised Jewish faces.

                                   Jesus came in.

A radiance so intense came forth from Him
that even I could feel it, far away.
Not dazzling light, but spirit, power and prayer.
He smiled in greeting and stretched out His hands.

The welcome guest. - And then I understood.
These were the men whom He had called His *friends*,
and with them were His kinsmen, down the ages,
before and after; from David until now.

They gave a Supper for Him, in love and worship.
Knowing Him truly, both as Man and God.
Of course, He had come first of all to them;
their family re-union was His Birthday-Feast.

THE GREAT LEAP
"Get your feet off the ground!

Didn't you know? - You died.

Clear the walls with a bound!

Come on up, - share the sound

and the joy of the singing,

where the firmament's ringing

and the air is wide."

FREESTYLE
Freedom means joining the dance,
the grand chain of all the stars;
where everyone knows the step,
and everyone's freelance.

Where motion and rest are one
and speed thrills in the cliffs;
where quietness is flight
and effort is gone.